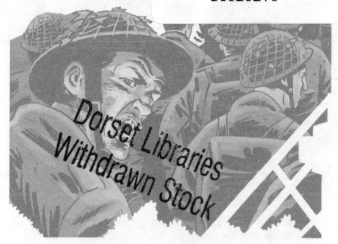

BRIDGE OF DEATH

Craig Simpson

Illustrated by Rob Davis and Geri Ford

First published in 2014
by Franklin Watts

Text © Craig Simpson 2014
Cover illustration by Rob Davis © Franklin Watts 2014
Interior illustrations by Geri Ford © Franklin Watts 2014
Cover design by Peter Scoulding

Franklin Watts
338 Euston Road
London NW1 3BH

Franklin Watts Australia
Level 17/207 Kent Street
Sydney, NSW 2000

A CIP catalogue record for this book
is available from the British Library.

(pb) ISBN: 978 1 4451 2387 5
(ebook) ISBN: 978 1 4451 2389 9
(Library ebook) ISBN: 978 1 4451 2391 2

1 3 5 7 9 10 8 6 4 2

Printed and bound by CPI Group (UK) Ltd, Croydon, CR0 4YY

Franklin Watts is a division of Hachette Children's Books,
an Hachette UK company.
www.hachette.co.uk

Contents

Chapter One
Cast Off

Major Drummond saw the pilot's signal. It was time to go to war. Darkness and low broken cloud hid the three Halifax bombers thundering southwards over the French coast. Explosions from the heavy flak of the German anti-aircraft guns below peppered the sky. Each bomber was using a tow rope a hundred yards long to pull a Horsa glider — their wooden airframes creaked and groaned under the strain. Inside each glider sat twenty-five terrified men in full combat uniform, crammed cheek by jowl, their faces blackened and their bowl-shaped helmets covered with camouflage netting. Their kit weighed in at over eighty pounds to a man, and each carried an equal weight of fear in his belly.

In One Dog, twenty-year-old Private Jack Riley sat with his back against the flimsy plywood and fabric-covered fuselage. The men were singing, but he was singing the loudest; more shouting than singing, trying to rid himself of the thought that within five minutes he might be dead. They might all be dead. The others in Jack's platoon were like brothers to him. They'd been training together day and night for months, and all for this one vital mission.

Several thousand feet below lay a bridge over a canal. It was heavily defended and rigged with explosives. Jack's platoon had to seize control of the bridge and hold it until reinforcements arrived. Jack knew that the element of surprise was everything.

If the enemy heard them coming they'd be slaughtered by machine-gun fire within seconds of landing. Jack tried to sing even louder.

Major Drummond bellowed at them to "Shut up!" Stooping, he moved unsteadily through the fuselage, issuing instructions. "Buckle up and brace for landing! Make sure your weapons are pointing down and safety catches are on! We don't want you blowing your own bleedin' heads off when we hit the ground, do we now?"

Interlinking arms, the soldiers clasped their hands tightly together in front of their chests. They also knew that if they hit the ground too hard the metal skid plate beneath the glider might explode up through the fuselage and crush their legs. So they crossed them and prepared to lift them into the air on the major's command.

The glider pilot reached down and seized a large red lever. He hesitated. This was it. All the months of training had been in preparation for this moment. Once he released the tow rope there was no going back. He took a deep breath and pulled. "Cast off!"

The droning engines of the Halifax tug faded as it headed off into the night, replaced by the howling roar of air rushing over the glider's wings and fuselage. Two Dog and Three Dog were following at one minute intervals. Together they carried a formidable force of men armed with Bren and Sten machine guns, mortars, grenades, PIAT rocket launchers, and a deep desire to hit the enemy hard.

Jack's thoughts turned to Mary, his girl back home. He had a photo of her tucked inside his tunic. She had no idea where he was. Just as well, Jack reckoned. He hated the thought of her worrying. Not that she had the slightest inkling he'd be one of the first soldiers on the ground. The long-awaited Allied invasion of mainland Europe had begun, the largest invasion in history and he, Jack Riley, was going to be there. He suddenly realised he was shaking uncontrollably. His mouth was dry too, so bone dry he could barely swallow.

The pilot pushed his control column forward and activated huge door-sized flaps on the wings, sending the wooden coffin into a steep, silent dive through the clouds, the altimeter spinning down rapidly.

Chapter Two
All Quiet

Dieter Kohl stepped out of his concrete pillbox and stretched the stiffness from his back. He emptied the dregs of cold coffee from his tin mug, and then went for a short stroll along the canal's towpath. He yawned from the boredom of manning his machine gun day after day, night after night, and for no good reason as far as he could see. Thirty men, he grumbled, wasting their lives, and all for one stupid bridge. He gazed at the metal structure that he'd grown to hate. He was both its protector and its prisoner. It was rigged with explosives and their orders were to blow it up if the British and Americans

ever came. Part of him wished they would. But he thought it unlikely. Rumours pointed to an invasion further east, nearer to Calais. If they did, though, then he could blow the bridge up and they could all go home. The thought cheered him up.

Dieter turned back and wandered onto the bridge, his ill-fitting boots clonking noisily. Halfway across he stopped, leant over the rail and peered down at the still water below. Music drifted through the air. There was a radio set playing in the slit trenches on his side of the canal, next to the road, boarding house and café-bar. He yawned again. Distant crumps and thuds of the coastal anti-aircraft batteries meant another air raid. It sounded far away. He wondered which German city would suffer that night. Berlin? Dresden? Cologne?

Germany was losing the war. Dieter knew that. Defeats in Russia and then North Africa meant the tide had turned. He looked up at the night sky: a black canvas, broken clouds, pinpricks of starlight. He blinked. Then he frowned. Was that a bird swooping in the distance? Hard to make out. He blinked again and narrowed his gaze. What sort of bird was it? It didn't look like any bird he knew. It seemed strangely rigid and was flying too straight. That's odd too, he observed, surprised that it appeared to be heading directly towards him.

Chapter Three
Sheer Terror

Jack's heart hammered fiercely in his chest. The swooping dive was like the mother of all big dippers. His ears began to hurt and his stomach did weird somersaults inside his belly, lurching up, then down, then sideways.

Corporal Bob Saunders was sitting next to Jack. They were good mates. Bob was the platoon's number one Bren machine gunner and was never short of a tall tale or rude joke. But now Bob was making strange groaning noises. As they fell out of the sky, Bob's head suddenly jolted forward and vomit spewed out of his mouth. In seconds they were all puking their guts up.

The whistling rush of wind grew louder, their airspeed higher, their angle of descent steeper. Filled with a growing panic, Jack desperately wanted to get out, to breathe fresh air, to feel the solid earth beneath his feet. *I don't want to die. Not like this. Not today.* Enemy bullets didn't worry him. Not yet. What made him pray like he'd never prayed before was the thought of what was coming next. To reach their target they first had to land. In the dark and in enemy territory, landing a glider really meant only one thing — crashing it.

Chapter Four
Hard and Fast

One Dog's pilot pulled back hard on the control column and wrestled the glider out of its dive at one thousand feet. He checked his compass and adjusted course. His co-pilot pressed his stopwatch. Tick...tick...tick...

"Five...four...three...two...one... Bingo!"

The pilot made a hard ninety-degree right-hand turn onto a new bearing and the co-pilot reset his stopwatch.

Tick...tick...tick... "Bingo!" ...and a second turn.

Now the canal lay dead ahead — a silvery thread — and the pilot could make out the bridge too. He glanced at his airspeed indicator: one hundred and twenty miles per hour. Way too fast. "We'll use the arrester parachute. Signal its release on my command."

The co-pilot nodded in readiness.

Jack knew the canal bridge was heavily defended. He'd seen the maps and photographs, and had studied the detailed scale model. There were two pillboxes, one either end of the bridge, and a system of trenches leading to a bunker. There were also anti-glider stakes scattered about, poking out of the ground, some quite close to the bridge and their LZ, the Landing Zone. The stakes were jokingly called "Rommel's Asparagus". Some joke, Jack thought. He hated asparagus.

Grasping a fuselage strut to steady

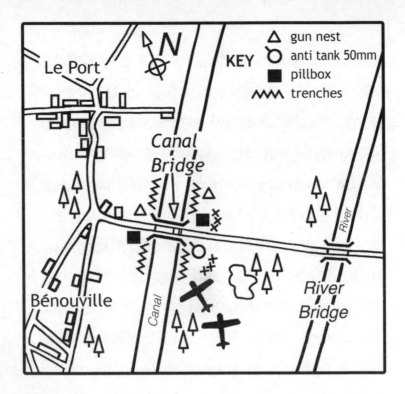

himself, Major Drummond opened the glider's side door and peered out just as it swooped silently over treetops, narrowly missing branches. Their closeness to the ground almost took his breath away. "Legs up, lads, and brace yourselves. We're going in."

One Dog's pilot held her steady

and aimed for the corner of the field. "Stream!" he called out, and the co-pilot raised a clenched fist. At the rear of the glider Private Munro released the arrester parachute; it tumbled out through a hatch in the floor, unfurled and snapped full of air. With a jolt the glider slowed and the nose dipped. "Jettison!" the pilot ordered, and the parachute was released. The canal and bridge still seemed to be racing towards them horribly fast. The pilot held his control column tightly. Sensing the ground rising up to greet them he closed his eyes and stiffened for impact.

One Dog smacked the ground hard at ninety miles per hour, nose wheel first, the pilot hurriedly jettisoning the main undercarriage by pulling a lever.

To Jack it sounded like the end of the world had come. The glider skidded along, weaving wildly, sparks flying up as the skid plate scraped over stony ground. Jack could see the sparks through the open door. He thought they were being shot at, the sparks tracer fire from enemy positions.

On and on they slid, bumping along, rocking, and slewing violently from side to side, men yelling and screaming in panic, fearful that the glider was breaking up. And it was. The nose wheel got wrenched off and the cockpit began to crumple. Then the glider pitched forward as it sank into a mass of coiled barbed wire. Cracks and snaps filled the air and were quickly joined by a hailstorm of splinters as

the cockpit shattered, propelling pilot
and co-pilot headfirst out of the glider.
They somersaulted through the air and
landed heavily. Both lay unconscious.
The glider ground to a stop just fifty
yards from the bridge.

Silence.

Men nursing bumps and bruises
regained their wits and began to groan
and curse. Harnesses clicked and Jack
sensed movement all around him in the
darkness.

"Everyone out! Out! Out! Out!"
shouted the major.

In what felt like a sea of bodies,
Jack stumbled out of the glider. He
tripped and landed on his stomach. He
struggled to his feet under the weight
of kit. Someone reached out and gave

him a hand. Winded, he fought to gasp air into his lungs. Jack mustered with the rest of his platoon beside one of the glider's wings. Clutching his Sten gun tightly, he dropped onto one knee and peered around. He realised in horror that the fuselage had split open close to the tail. A lucky escape.

Bob Saunders's blackened face emerged from the darkness in front of Jack. "Ammo clips, Jack. For the Bren. Give them to me. Quickly!"

Each man carried four clips of ammo for the Bren guns. Fumbling, Jack reached for his. Bob snatched them from Jack's hand and within seconds had set up his Bren on a tripod just five yards away.

Two Dog swooped in and landed

behind them. Slamming into an unsuspecting cow, it slewed hard to the left, crashed through a hedge and slid into a nearby pond. Men tumbled out, dazed and shaken, wading and splashing about utterly disorientated. With the glider's nose submerged, Jack feared for the fate of the pilot.

"Get a move on," snapped the major. Jack felt the major's hand on his shoulder. "We've got to take the bridge."

Up on his feet, Jack ran blindly towards the canal. The silhouette of the bridge loomed like a sleeping dragon. Men were charging alongside Jack, Lance Corporal Billy Sawyer to his left and Sergeant Lee Parks to his right, their breathing heavy, their backpacks

slapping with each stride. The major led from the front. Jack felt a thrilling surge of euphoria, despite his legs feeling like jelly. He'd made it down! He was alive! He'd defied the cold hand of death. Now, as the bridge drew close, he'd have to defy it once again.

Not a shot had been fired. They had achieved the element of surprise. Jack couldn't believe their luck. Their crazy plan actually seemed to be working. As he ran, stumbling across the uneven stony field, he heard the thud of Three Dog landing behind him, and the hideous noise of splintering wood suggesting it had come down far too fast and hard.

Chapter Five
Panic Stations!

Dieter Kohl was running. Just moments before he'd stood, frozen in disbelief, as the wooden bird had silently glided out of the sky like a giant eagle and landed just fifty yards from the bridge. And there were others. He'd spotted at least two more.

No one reacted. Was he the only one who'd seen the enemy arrive?

Terrified, he stumbled down the steps into his pillbox and shook awake the young private who'd been curled up beneath a blanket. "Jurgen! Wake up. We are being attacked."

Bleary-eyed, Jurgen Klein, a seventeen-year-old conscript, anxiously scrambled to his feet and reached for his helmet and rifle. Confusion was written all over his face. Was old Dieter playing another of his silly pranks on him? It wouldn't be the first time. Dieter liked poking fun and practical jokes.

"Here, take this, go outside and fire a flare into the air," Dieter barked, handing the confused young man a flare pistol. "And then run to the trench and make sure the radio operator in the bunker alerts High Command. Tell them they've come in gliders and we need reinforcements from the garrison at Caen. Better still, tell them to send an entire panzer division. There's one based not far away, south of here. And then blow the bridge. *Schnell, Jurgen, Schnell!*"

Flummoxed and still unsure whether old Dieter was being serious, Jurgen stood indecisively still, not budging an inch. Dieter grabbed hold of him and shoved him up the steps. "Go! You must blow the bridge. And for God's sake keep your head down."

Dieter then hurriedly turned and positioned himself behind his tripod-

mounted MG 42 belt-fed machine gun.
He pressed the stock into his shoulder
and peered along the barrel, through
the pillbox's narrow firing slit, to the
world beyond. He'd never felt such
a rush of energy. He'd never felt so
alive...and so scared. Considering
the enemy were almost upon him it
remained eerily silent outside. He
paused a second to wonder if it had all
been a horrible dream. Then he spotted
shadows moving in a nearby field and
he was certain they weren't cattle.
They were too small. And there were
too many of them. Dieter took aim.

Chapter Six
The Element of Surprise

Major Drummond led the silent charge to within thirty feet of the bridge, then suddenly dipped left and flung himself down against a steep, grassy embankment. Within five seconds Jack and four others were beside him.

"Sawyer and Parks take up positions behind the bridge's pillars this end and cover us. Riley, I've got a special little job for you, lad."

"Sir?" Jack didn't like the sound of that.

"Clear the pillbox this side of the bridge. We can't move until it's been dealt with. Do it just like you did in training. Sneak up and lob a grenade into it."

Jack gulped. The last thirty feet looked horribly exposed to enemy fire.

"Well don't just sit there like a lemming, get a move on."

Jack crawled forward on his hands and knees, his pulse racing. Lying flat, he reached for a grenade and tore out the pin with his teeth.

As soon as the grenade exploded, the major tore off towards the bridge, pistol drawn. Jessop and Carver were at his shoulder, both brandishing their Sten guns. They hammered onto the forty yard span, yelling their heads off in a well-rehearsed battle cry. They spotted a soldier at the far end and began firing.

Jurgen Klein fumbled with his flare pistol. He'd never actually fired one before. He heard shouting on the bridge. He heard boots stomping. He saw figures, frightening shadows in the dark. Dieter hadn't been playing a trick after all, he realised. They really were under attack! Trembling, he quickly pointed the flare pistol into the sky. The first bullet hit him in the belly, the second in the shoulder. He staggered to his right. Another bullet hit him in the chest. He pulled the trigger as he fell. A fourth bullet tore straight through his helmet in a spray of pink mist. The flare shot high into the sky and began to arc, burning brightly.

Dieter Kohl opened up with his MG 42 machine gun, nicknamed the Hitlersäge, or Hitler's Saw. A formidable weapon, it was able to fire up to fifteen hundred rounds per minute, a rate so fast it sounded like a chainsaw. Dieter began with short bursts, aimed at the fields. Having seen the pillbox explode at the other end of the bridge, he swung the barrel round and aimed along the span. He saw shapes moving. He gritted his teeth and let rip.

41

Chapter Seven
Glory Dash

Sergeant Todd swore loudly when he heard the major was trapped. Then he barked a string of orders. "Bring up one of our Brens and focus firing on the trench system that leads off the towpath and into the bunker. If anything pops up, blast it to hell. And hurry up with that PIAT rocket launcher. That other pillbox has to be silenced or the bridge will remain a killing zone for the enemy." Todd peered down the line of men crouched up against the embankment. "Where are our sappers?"

"Here, sir." The five engineers crawled forward.

"Get going. You've got to cut any

fuse wires before they have a chance
to blow the bridge. We'll cover you."

Under suppressing fire from Jack
and his platoon, the engineers crept
forward towards the bridge. Sawyer
and Parks were still in position at the
end of the bridge, and trying to figure
out how to get the major back safely.
The major was still lying flat halfway

across the bridge and bellowing insults at the enemy beyond.

"Hold your position. They're going to try taking out that machine gun," said one sapper encouragingly to a terrified-looking Lance Corporal Billy Sawyer. He pointed to the pillbox where Dieter was rapidly running low on ammo. "Then the major can risk crawling back."

Billy nodded.

The sappers crept down under the bridge, clambered onto the struts and began hauling themselves out over the canal, their fingers trying to detect telltale fuse wires in the dark. Using their wire clippers they cut them all, edging further and further along. To be sure, they knew they'd have to crawl all the way across.

"Where's that blasted PIAT?" yelled Sergeant Todd, in exasperation.

"Shan't be a tick, sir," came the reply.

An anti-tank weapon, the PIAT rocket launcher was also perfect for taking out a concrete pillbox. A short spring-loaded launch tube supported on a monopod fired three-pound hollow-charge bombs, effective up to ninety yards. As Private Ned Jenkins took aim, he reckoned the pillbox couldn't be more than thirty yards away. "Carefully does it, now," he muttered quietly to himself, concentrating hard amid the unfolding chaos around him. "Nice and easy. Let's see if I can get a hole in one."

Chapter Eight
The Final Push

Dieter Kohl wiped the sweat from his brow. He had lain down such a continuous blanket of fire that he was running low on ammo — perhaps only enough for another fifteen seconds of

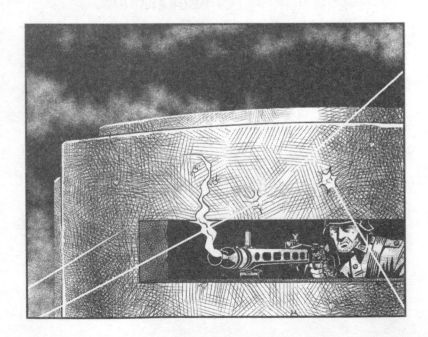

continuous fire. The barrel of his MG 42 was so hot it needed replacing, too. He now had a tough decision to make. Changing the barrel would take seconds, grabbing and inserting the last of his ammo belts a few seconds more. His ears were ringing. To carry on was pointless. He was outnumbered. Soon he'd be outgunned. He felt defeated. He made up his mind and abandoned the gun, scrambling quickly towards the pillbox's sunken entrance. He grabbed his rifle on the way out. He'd decided to take his chances out in the open. Maybe he could try to get away and rendezvous with reinforcements. Emerging, he crawled into some thick bushes and headed off into the night.

Sergeant Todd peered into the dark, adding, "That was a bloody good shot."

"Thank you, sir. It was me, Private Jenkins."

"Well done. Just one thing, Jenkins."

"What's that, sir?"

"Next time, Jenkins, try not to take all bloody day about it."

"Right-oh, sir."

"Now, men, let's secure this bridge." Todd rose to his feet and waved the platoon forward.

Within seconds they were all running, all yelling. Jack was in the midst of them. He fizzed with a toxic mix of fear and excitement that made his legs wobble and his brain feel light-headed. Would he get shot? Would the bridge blow up?

Chapter Nine
The Longest Ten Minutes

Their boots thundered over the metal grids covering the bridge. Enemy tracer fire flashed. Bullets pinged. Still they ran, shouting and yelling, spraying short bursts of fire from their Sten machine guns. Others flung grenades. Someone let out a cry and fell. Still they ran.

As they reached the major, he rose up and joined their charge. Jack leaped over the lifeless body of Private Carver.

Still they ran, until safely on the other side. They divided into small groups, one fanning right, one left, one heading straight on. Jack's lot went left, sped down to the towpath beside

the canal and, as they ran, they flung
grenades into the shadows of the slit
trenches. Five grenades, five flashes,
five explosions.

Jack jumped down into the trench
in search of the concealed bunker. He
edged forward, ready to fire. Bodies
lay everywhere, some beneath his
feet, others leaning up against the side

of the trench. He pressed on. Steps led down. He'd found the bunker. He yanked the pin from a grenade and tossed it through the doorway. A flash and a bang knocked Jack off his feet. He scrambled back up. "Bunker clear!"

It was over, Jack realised. They'd taken the bridge. He sat down on the ground and glanced at his watch. He was shaking so much he had trouble reading it. The luminescent dial glowed in the night. He stared at it. Ten minutes! That's all it had taken since the glider landed. Ten minutes to capture the bridge.

"Well done, lads, time to secure the perimeter," yelled the major. "You all know what to do. Set up defensive positions, and do a sweep of the area.

Check every building, outhouse, privy, tree, ditch and under every bush." The major spun on his heels. "Now, where's the radio operator? We've got to send the good news to HQ."

Men from Two and Three Dog who'd survived their landings arrived in numbers, and quickly set up their Brens and PIATs where, just minutes earlier, the positions had been occupied by the enemy. Jack took a moment to inspect the remains of the pillbox: all rubble and dust and the twisted remains of a barrel. He kicked a few stones aside, expecting to see a German uniform, a lifeless hand, maybe an entire dead body. But there was nothing.

"Hey, Jack, come on, we're going to check out that café."

Jack hurried off to join his mates who were hammering their fists on the door to the shuttered French café-bar. One of a handful of buildings, it appeared deserted, but then they heard a sound from above. They took a few steps back and peered up at a first floor window. A curtain had been pulled back. Jack snatched his Sten to his shoulder and aimed at it.

The window swung open and an elderly man's face appeared. He gazed down at their blackened faces quizzically.

"*Français?*" someone enquired.

"*Oui,*" then, in English with a strong French accent, the old café owner added, "Of course I'm French. This is France!"

"What he means is are there any Germans inside?" Jack shouted.

The old man shook his head.

"We have to check." Jack gestured to the door. "Open up. Or we'll kick it down."

Chapter Ten
The Long Wait

Dieter Kohl collapsed, exhausted, in a ditch beneath a hedge. He'd been crawling for ages. The quiet told him that the fighting was over. But who'd won? Had anyone seen the flare? If they had, where were the reinforcements?

Jack waited nervously on the bridge. It had been over an hour since they'd captured it, and they should have been relieved by now. The major stuck close to the radio operator and messages seemed to be going back and forth, each more confused than the last. Then someone yelled, "Enemy patrol boat!"

The boat's engine coughed and spluttered. Then the boat turned round and headed away. Jack joined in with the cheers from the rest of his platoon.

Jack gazed up at the sky. More waiting, more listening out for the enemy. He longed for the approaching dawn, and thought about the hundreds of thousands of troops who'd soon be wading ashore on the Normandy beaches. And of the paratroopers dropping inland. He felt sure it was the beginning of the end of the war. And he'd been there. He'd help secure a route for British troops inland. Securing the bridge was vital.

Someone shouted out. Everyone leaped to their feet. Jack heard them coming too. From the road to the north. Everyone began cheering and waving their helmets in the air. Jack's weariness was replaced by elation. Reinforcements had arrived! Soon he'd be able to stand down, get something to eat and then some well-earned shut-eye. And then, thought Jack, we'll press on, all the way to Berlin.

Dieter Kohl crawled and crawled, his chin in the dirt, cutting across a field of potatoes towards the next village. Not far now, he thought. Still no sign of reinforcements. He'd hoped to hear the rumble of tanks along the country lanes, the stomp of boots of men marching in columns, or the clatter of trucks and artillery. Where were they? Why hadn't they come?

The faintest light of dawn lit the horizon in the east. Dieter paused to wipe the sweat from his brow with a grubby hand.

Aircraft! He could hear aircraft! He rolled over onto his back and stared into the sky. He blinked. Was he dreaming? Above him, hundreds of parachutes were drifting down towards him. He scrambled to his feet, and turned, spinning round and round until giddy, all the time peering towards the heavens.

With Allied paratroopers landing all around him, Dieter dropped his rifle, raised his hands into the air and then placed them on his head. Soldiers began running towards him. He sunk onto his knees. This is it, he thought,

as they surrounded him, shouting and swearing and shoving the barrels of their weapons into his back and chest. Either I'm about to die, or God willing one day soon this nightmare will finally be over and I can go home.

Author's Note

Although a work of fiction, *Bridge of Death* is inspired by a real D-Day mission called Operation Deadstick. In the hours before Allied troops landed on the Normandy beaches, key bridges over the Caen canal (including Pegasus Bridge) and the River Orne had to be seized intact. Responsibility fell to the 2nd Battalion, Oxford and Buckinghamshire Light Infantry, Royal Engineers, and aircrew from the Glider Pilot Regiment. This night-time *coup de main* (surprise attack) was an incredible success, not least owing to the glider pilots who demonstrated some of the most phenomenal flying skills seen during the war, landing their Horsa gliders close to their targets. By capturing and securing these bridges Allied troops landing on "Sword" beach had an accessible route inland to the east.

BATTLE BOOKS

BY GARY SMAILES

Take up your weapons and prepare to fight your own
battle in these choose-your-own-destiny books!

978 1 4451 0112 5 pb
978 1 4451 0839 1 ebook

978 1 4451 0113 2 pb
978 1 4451 0840 7 ebook

978 1 4451 0114 9 pb
978 1 4451 0841 4 ebook

978 1 4451 0115 6 pb
978 1 4451 0842 1 ebook